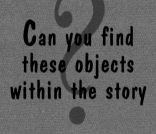

Can you find these objects within the story?

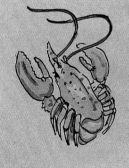

THE TWO TRAILS

A TREASURE TREE
ADVENTURE

BY **JOHN TRENT, Ph.D.** ILLUSTRATED BY **JUDY LOVE**

Tommy
NELSON

Thomas Nelson, Inc.

Nashville

To three priceless, precious young ladies who are also life-long friends, Brynne Abraham, Laura Trent, and Kari Trent. You were my captive audience and invaluable "kid critics" when we drove to school. You were also the first to cheer when the "Bungee Bears" came to the rescue, and laugh about "Turtle Tag." Mom and I are so proud of the choices you've made as you've grown up, and the trail you've chosen to head toward God's best.
—JOHN TRENT

To Alan—
who has cheered me on throughout our many years together, my heartfelt appreciation for your artistic guidance and loving support during the creation of this book.
—JUDY LOVE

Published in Nashville, Tennessee, by Tommy Nelson™, a division of Thomas Nelson, Inc.

Executive Editor: Laura Minchew
Managing Editor: Beverly Phillips

Library of Congress Cataloging-in-Publication-Data

Trent, John T.
  The two trails / by John Trent.
     p. cm.
  Continues the adventures of the four best friends begun in The treasure tree.
  Summary: Owl's birthday gift sends four animal friends on an adventure that helps them to appreciate the qualities that make them individuals.
  ISBN 0-8499-1450-7
  [1. Individuality—Fiction. 2. Friendship—Fiction. 3. Animals—Fiction.]
I. Title.
PZ7.T71945Tw 1998
[E]—dc21

                                                                97-11118
                                                                  CIP
                                                                  AC

Printed in the United States of America
98 99 00 01 02 03 RRD 9 8 7 6 5 4 3 2 1

Letter to Parents

The idea for this book wasn't hard to come up with, since I've had a *lifetime* of experience in dealing with "opposites"! You see, I'm a twin. When people would meet Jeff and me, they'd assume because the "outside" looked so similar, we'd be mirror images in our attitudes and actions, but we were opposites.

Jeff was like Chewy the Beaver. He has *always* been organized and concerned with details. (He's now an outstanding cancer doctor at the National Institute of Health.) For example, as a child he had a sock drawer with all the same color socks neatly rolled up and put away. Unfortunately, I was his roommate and I didn't have a sock drawer, I had a sock "room"! (I was like Giggles!)

Today, my wife, Cindy, and I have two precious daughters who look like they came from the same cookie-cutter, yet they have very different personalities.

If you've got "opposites" in your home, *The Two Trails* provides a warm, fun lesson in appreciating differences, and learning how "opposites" can become close friends. This story continues the friends' adventures begun in *The Treasure Tree*. This time, the friends split into two teams that follow two adventurous trails and learn to love and appreciate each other's differences.

Learning to live in harmony with an "opposite" is an important life lesson for children. They'll be dealing with many opposites throughout the years . . . and you never know . . . they might just marry an opposite.

John Trent, Ph.D.
President,
Encouraging Words

Another Great Adventure Begins . . .

It seemed hard to believe, but an entire *year* had passed since the four best friends' last adventure. Their last adventure had begun at a birthday party . . . and so too would this one.

Of course, you remember the four best friends. Chewy is the very organized and detailed Beaver. Lance is the take-charge, "I can do it!" Lion. Honey is the warm, sensitive, always-ready-to-listen Golden Retriever. And Giggles is the "party-waiting-to-happen," fun-loving Otter.

Chapter One

The four friends *always* celebrated their birthdays together. And this year was no exception. In fact, their birthday party was the talk of the forest!

There were balloons and surprises, and a game that was a forest favorite, called "Tag the Turtle." Now, playing tag with a turtle might *sound* like an easy game. But in this forest, the turtle gets to wear four jet-powered Rollerblades!

But the high point of the party was the scrumptious cake Chewy's mother had made. Everyone knows Beavers bake the best chocolate cakes in the forest (because they follow all the directions and bake it "just right"). This cake was so big, rich, and tasty that the best friends would *still* be eating cake if Wise Old Owl hadn't interrupted with an exciting announcement.

I've got a gift for you to open!" cried Wise Old Owl excitedly.

"Oh, you *shouldn't* have," said Honey, the sensitive Golden Retriever.

"If you count last year's gift, that's two gifts from you, Owl!" said Chewy Beaver excitedly. *"Ah . . . But who's counting,"* the Beaver said shyly. (Actually, Chewy shouldn't have been embarrassed. Beavers are good at counting and remembering things.)

"Does this mean another adventure's afoot?" asked Lance the Lion eagerly. (Lions can't wait for another adventure. In fact, they've even been known to *cause* an adventure if one doesn't come along soon enough!)

"What was that? *Who's got Jell-O on his foot?"* asked Giggles, the fun-loving Otter. Giggle's hadn't heard Lance quite right because somehow while eating she'd managed to get chocolate cake in both of her ears!

The four best friends quickly gathered around Wise Old Owl and opened their present. The last present they'd opened from Owl had contained a map. But what Chewy held up now was something quite different.

This time the Beaver held up a beautiful globe. Actually, there were two globes in the box. Each was the size of a very large Christmas ornament, yet crystal clear. Clear, that is, except for some beautiful writing, and a single red "X" on each globe. Upon closer inspection, each held its own message. Something that sounded much like a riddle, and very much like the start of another adventure.

These are the words they found on the first globe:

Two friends must team up, right from the start,
one full of strength, one with sensitive heart.
Straight up you'll shoot to where "X" marks the spot,
and not end until a great battle is fought.

With a pawshake, Lance the Lion and Honey the
Golden Retriever agreed to travel one road to adventure
together.

The message on the second globe read:

> *Two friends it takes to follow path two,*
> *a mixture of good sense and good humor too!*
> *Straight down you will go until you see stars;*
> *you won't stop until something falls from afar.*

The second riddle took a bit more time to agree on. That's because Chewy Beaver firmly insisted that the instructions said, "good humor" and that Giggle's jokes could hardly be called, "good." (Particularly because Giggle's had just told the joke about how *five* was scared of *six* . . . because *seven eight nine!*) But in the end, they all saw through the Beaver's kidding, and it was settled—Chewy and Giggles would set out together on this path.

Two unlikely pairs would travel two very different
trails. They didn't know it yet, but each trail would bring
them face to face with danger, and closer to each other
than ever before. But no one was getting started until
they'd all sampled just a bit more of Mamma Beaver's
delicious chocolate cake!

Packing for an Adventure

It took some doing to prepare for their new adventure.

Lance was ready in a heartbeat, carrying his small pack that included "just the basics." (Things like barbells to work out with, several energy bars, and four of his many swimming medals. These medals were to remind him if things got tough, *"I can do it!"*)

Honey took much longer to pack because she had to say goodbye to so many friends. (And she had so many addresses to get in case she had time to write.)

Chewy also spent a long time packing. That's because he first had to make a *list* of what he should take, and then carefully clean, pack, and "double check" each item off his list!

. . . And then there was Giggles the Otter. Long after
everyone else was ready, Giggles ran up shouting, *"I can't
find my pack!* . . . Wait a minute!" she said, using her Otter
sense of creativity. "This will work just as well!" And
Giggles proudly began stuffing a large yellow paper sack
with three socks (all different colors), two of her favorite
hats (she wore her favorite one that looked like a smiling
fish), and one of her favorite "Adventures in Odyssey"
tapes. (The fact that she wasn't bringing a tape player
didn't matter. She just *loved* those tapes!)

11

And so it was, on a beautiful summer morning, that the four best friends touched paws, and set off for an adventure. Two friends down each trail—different as can be—following the globes that would be their maps.

Climbing Mount Eagle-Eye-In-The-Sky

Do you remember the first riddle that paired up the Lion and Golden Retriever? It went:

Two friends must team up, right from the start,
one full of strength, one with sensitive heart.
Straight up you'll shoot to where "X" marks the spot,
and not end until a great battle is fought.

As Lance and Honey studied their globe, they noticed that the spot the "X" marked seemed to float *above* the globe. Without hesitation, Lance made a decision. "That 'X' has to be Mount Eagle-Eye-In-The-Sky. It's the highest place in the entire forest. That's got to be it!"

Chapter Three

A shudder went down Honey's back all the way to the tip of her tail. "But no one's ever climbed Mount Eagle-Eye-In-The-Sky . . . or at least they've never come back to tell about it!" exclaimed Honey.

"Which is just another reason why this is going to be such a great adventure!" Lance said confidently. "We'll be the first ones to set our paws on its peak—I'm sure that's the spot with the 'X'!" And without another word he turned and started walking quickly down the road to "high" adventure.

If you've sensed that Lions and Golden Retrievers make decisions differently, you're right. Lance made his decision quickly, without much discussion or sharing with his friend. Honey, on the other hand, wanted to talk to Lance more about where they were going. However, she ran out of breath trying to catch up with him to talk!

As they hurried toward the looming Mount Eagle-Eye-In-The-Sky, there were more differences between them that began to surface. In fact, one difference got them in terrible trouble—but moved them closer to "X" marks the spot.

After a long march, they finally reached the foot of the mountain, and Lance called a "time out" for lunch. They both sat down to enjoy their sandwiches. That's when a problem arose.

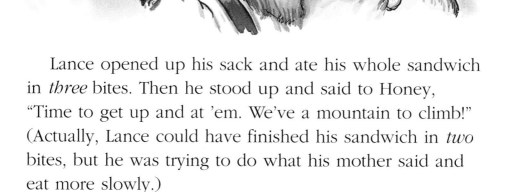

Lance opened up his sack and ate his whole sandwich in *three* bites. Then he stood up and said to Honey, "Time to get up and at 'em. We've a mountain to climb!" (Actually, Lance could have finished his sandwich in *two* bites, but he was trying to do what his mother said and eat more slowly.)

"We just sat down!" said Honey, who had only eaten part of her lunch. (Golden Retrievers like to talk about their day when they eat lunch, not hurry through it in three bites.) Honey stood and held up her sandwich to show Lance she'd just started to eat, but this turned out to be a nearly disastrous thing to do.

Circling high above them, a humongous, bald eagle
(bigger than your front door!) spotted Honey's sandwich
held high in the air. The eagle swooped down to grab
it . . . but instead of getting just the sandwich, it clasped
Honey's paw as well. With an ear-splitting eagle scream
and a blinding flash of feathers, the eagle took off with
Honey's lunch—and Honey!

19

How Lance kept his wits during this time was a tribute to his "quick thinking" Lion ability. Instead of panicking, he instantly turned and ran ahead of the slow-flying eagle and climbed a towering Pine. Then with a leap off the top branch that would have won first place at anyone's field day festivities, he grabbed hold of Honey. But instead of rescuing her, he could only hold on as the eagle proceeded to lazily carry *both* of them up and up and up!

Things looked *terrible* for the two friends as they dangled hundreds of feet above the treetops. And to make things worse, the eagle appeared to be taking them right toward a sheer rock cliff at the top of Mount Eagle-Eye-In-The-Sky! They'd be crushed against the mountain, or worse still, dropped to the forest below!

But at the last possible moment, the eagle gave one last flap of her huge wings. Up they shot to a single branch springing from the rocky cliff with an eagle's nest built on top of it. A nest filled with three curious—*and very hungry*—eaglets. With a bounce, Lance and Honey dropped into the nest, and when they sat up, four pairs of eagle eyes were looking right at them.

It was Honey who saved the day. She could tell the eagles were nice eagles. (Don't ask me how. Golden Retrievers just *know* those sorts of things about others.) As carefully as she could, she took the sandwich she was still holding, and broke it into four parts. She placed one in front of each eagle, who eyed her a moment before gobbling up the snack.

"Look in your pack!" said Honey. "They're hungry. Let's share our food with them!"

And Lance and Honey made the eagles a feast from the food they'd brought.

Everything was going well until they started eating Lance's bubble gum for dessert. Having eaten so much and so fast, one of the eaglets got the hiccups, and out popped a bubble gum bubble. Then the mother eagle hiccuped and out popped a *big* bubble. And, quick as a wink, *all the eagles* began blowing and popping huge bubbles!

It's hard not to become friends with someone you've popped bubbles with. And to cement their friendship, (as if the bubble gum weren't sticky enough), Honey whispered something to Lance. Instantly he nodded his head, called for everyone's attention, and made an announcement.

"Eagle friends," he said. "For taking us so far on our journey to *'X' marks the spot*, there's something we'd like to present to you."

While Honey hummed the Forest National Anthem, the eagles stood as proud as eagles can stand as the two friends awarded Lance's gold swimming medal to the mother eagle. Then each of the three baby eagles received one of his bronze medals. (Don't worry, Lance had *lots* of medals. And besides, Honey's sensitive idea to say "thank you" in a special way had made the eagles so happy that Lance was surprised he hadn't thought of it himself!)

Then, like the "group hug" you get when your cousins show up at your door from across the country, the four eagles gathered around Lance and Honey and gently put their wings around them. They got an "eagle hug." So soft and warm, it makes hugging your feather pillow seem like hugging a rock.

What the two friends didn't know was that something new was about to fall their way . . . literally! We'll find out what that "something" was, but first, let's peek down the other trail. After a late start (Otters are *notorious* for starting late; something that didn't make Chewy Beaver happy at all), this unlikely pair had started down their trail—*and right into an adventure of their own.*

Bottom Side Up!

While Lance and Honey were high up in the mountains with eagles, Chewy the Beaver and Giggles the Otter were having an adventure as well. In case you don't remember, the riddle on their globe read:

> *Two friends it takes to follow path two,*
> *a mixture of good sense and good humor too!*
> *Straight down you will go until you see stars;*
> *You won't stop until something falls from afar.*

As the Beaver and Otter looked at their globe, their "X" seemed to rest right in the middle of the ocean!

"There must be an island there," said Chewy (always good at thinking practically about things). "Otherwise the 'X' would be floating instead of standing still."

"Whatever!" said Giggles. "I'm ready to swim there!" And so she was. She'd already dug into her sack and put on her new blue swimsuit, her favorite dinosaur "floatie" toy, and her swim goggles.

Chapter Four

"*Giggles,*" said Chewy, "it's too far to swim, even for an Otter. We'll have to go by boat."

Now, if you can't go for a swim, then going on a boat ride is just as much fun. So without hesitation the two friends hurried down to the seashore, and ran right into disappointment. For not a single captain in the harbor was willing to go on an adventure.

There were dozens of brightly colored ships all right. But every one was either too small, or its crew was too afraid to head off on a long journey. Just when it looked like they might have to give up the trail altogether, an old Sea Parrot spoke up from its perch on the wharf.

"*Akkkk* . . . Ye be looking for a ship for a long, perilous adventure, be ye?" asked the Parrot.

"Oh, yes!" said the friends.

"Well then, maties, there's only one place to go. Only one captain's brave and clever enough, and only one ship's fast enough for your needs. Look for a classy sloop at the far end of the pier called the *Bottom-Side-Up* and the salty old sea dog named Stop who's the captain. They'll both do you proud!"

Right away, Chewy didn't like the name of the ship, and he said so. For while Beavers are excellent swimmers, everyone knows that on boat trips, you don't want to even *think* about the "bottom side" of the boat coming up. But Giggles had already run ahead down the pier, excited about seeing the ship.

Only when they got there, it didn't look like any ship they'd ever seen. Instead of having a large, square sail like all the other ships, this ship had a single, huge, rainbow-colored, *circular* sail in the middle of its deck. And at the back of the ship, above and behind the ship's wheel, there was a giant fan with blades as big as airplane propellers.

The Captain wasn't exactly what they expected either. The "salty old sea dog" that greeted them wasn't a dog at all—*it was a chicken!*

Now Chewy was *really* concerned.

"Giggles," the worried Beaver said, pulling his friend aside. "Do you think it's a good idea to go to sea with a *chicken* for a captain?"

"Sure!" said Giggles, jumping aboard the ship. "You've never heard of 'Chicken of the Sea'?"

The two of them jumped on board, and quick as a wink, Captain Stop agreed to take them to where the 'X' rested in the middle of the ocean. "Get yourselves something to hold on to!" cried the chicken. "Let's cast off and be on our way!"

The sea gull, who was first mate, untied the ship from the pier and raised the anchor. The captain pulled a chain that turned on the huge fan.

"We're off!" shouted Captain Stop, holding on to his hat.

"Here we go, Stop!" cried the excited Giggles in reply.

"*All stop!*" said the Captain, shutting off the fan and dropping the anchor.

"No, *go,* Stop!" said Giggles.

"All ahead full!" cried the confused chicken, starting the fan again as the sea gull frantically pulled up the anchor.

"That's it, Stop!"
"Crash stop!" said
the chicken, throwing
everyone forward as
the boat slid to a stop.

"No, *go*, Stop!"
yelled Giggles.

Chances are they would
have gone the whole trip
sprinting ahead and then
coming to a crashing stop,
if Chewy Beaver hadn't
put a stop to all the
stopping.

"Giggles," said the frustrated Beaver, "just call him *'Captain,'* instead of 'Stop'!"

"Oh! That makes sense!" said Giggles (who had actually enjoyed being thrown back and forth). "Let's go, Captain!" she said.

And in a flash they were off!

Like a roller coaster, the *Bottom-Side-Up* would shoot up a wave and soar high in the air, only to fall back down into the water before climbing the next wave.

Chewy Beaver was hanging on to the mast for dear life, thinking of an "abandon ship" plan just in case they needed one. (Beavers like to be prepared for possible emergencies!) However, Giggles was busy exploring the ship. That's when she saw and . . . *without thinking of the consequences* . . . pushed the large red button on the ship's mast.

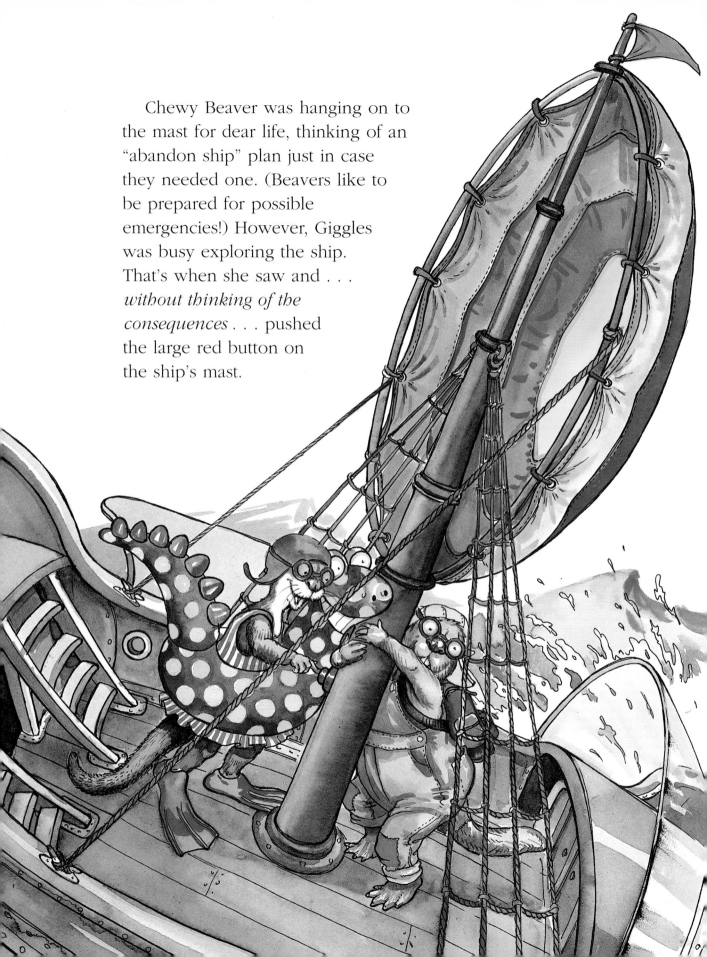

Instantly, the colored sail folded up . . .

and a clear thick plastic cover (like half an eggshell) snapped up around the entire ship!

Without knowing it, Giggles had pushed the "bottom-side-up" button!

The ship was in midair when
Giggles pushed the button. When it came
down this time, instead of landing *on top* of
the water—the ship plowed down deep *into* the sea!
Captain Stop's ship was actually a rare, experimental
version of a combination speedboat/submarine!

38

And while Captain Stop had never actually *tried* the
experiment, it was working perfectly. The huge fan that
had once filled the sail with air, now turned outward and
became a propeller! And as quickly as they had skimmed
across the sea, they were now shooting down . . . down
. . . down toward the bottom of the sea!

"This is great!" cried Giggles,
watching confused fish scurry out of
the way as the submarine raced downward.

"It *would be great*, if I knew how to turn off the
fan!" shouted Captain Stop.

"We're going to crash!" cried Chewy, looking at the
ocean floor rushing up at them! And they were. They
were racing straight toward the bottom at full speed.

Was their trail about to end in tragedy?

Fantastic Fun in Cloudville

We'll find out what happened to Giggles and Chewy shortly. But first let's return to our other pair of opposites. When we left Lance and Honey, they were in the middle of a "group hug" from some very large eagles. That's when an even bigger part of the adventure happened.

In all the commotion of being dropped in the nest, laying out a small feast for their new friends, blowing bubbles together, and having an awards ceremony, no one saw what was approaching. And the "what" was a cloud.

Chapter Five

And it was no ordinary cloud. When you go outside, clouds can pass over you all day and you barely notice them. But when you're at the top of a mountain and a cloud is ready to bump into you—*it's hard not to notice.*

Just as the eagles were giving Lance and Honey their softest hug ever, the cloud bumped into the mountain and something fell out. That something had a long cord attached to it, and it dropped right into Lance's arms. "It" was a small white bear, as fluffy as the cloud it had just fallen from. And it was sound asleep! Attached to the bear was a long bungee cord that stretched back up into the cloud!

Now, you know what happens when a bungee cord is *reeeeeeeallllllly* stretched. That's right! It snaps back! And as Lance held the little sleeping bear, it was Honey's turn to see what was happening, and try to rescue Lance.

"Let go of that bear!" cried Honey as she wrapped her arms around the two of them . . . but it was too late. With a "poof!" that happened in the blink of an eye, Lance, Honey and the sleeping bear shot up right into the middle of the cloud . . . and disappeared!

For those of you who aren't familiar with "bungee bears," perhaps I should explain. You see, all those summer days when you've looked up at huge, white, puffy clouds, you may have missed something. That's understandable. You've always been looking at the *bottom* of clouds.

On *top* of certain clouds are "bungee bear cities!" (Not *all* clouds of course! Otherwise you'd see bungee bears when you looked out the window on airplane trips.) The tops of bungee clouds are filled with snow-white bungee bears.

And every bungee bear has one thing in common. Namely, they each have a long bungee cord attached to them. That way, if a cloud bumps into a mountain (or a very tall building), bears near the edge of the cloud don't have to worry about falling off. The bungee cord just lets them fall until it's all stretched out, then it springs them back to Cloudville—*and right into the arms of their mothers!*

That's just what had happened to the bear Lance and Honey were holding! This bear (named Noodles) had indeed fallen off the cloud. Now his cord snapped back and sent the bungee bear—along with a very surprised Lance and Honey—flying. That is, until they landed on top of an even *more* surprised mother bear!

Now it just so happened that out of all the bungee bears on all the bungee clouds, there was *one* bear with a very distinctive birthmark on her stomach. *You guessed it.* Noodle's mom was born with a very large "X" on her large, white stomach. And the three flying animals had landed right on the X!

"I've done it!" shouted Lance. For indeed, just like the riddle, they had landed on "X" marks the spot! Lance forgot that Honey did as much to find the spot as he did. But Honey quickly forgave Lance for not thinking of her.

When they looked around, they saw that all the bungee bears from the entire city had crowded around them.

"Remember the
last part of the riddle?" asked Honey.

"I sure do," said Lance. "Our adventure won't end
'until a great battle is fought.'"

"Do you think we're about to be in that great
battle?" asked Honey breathlessly. She had never been in
a battle, and certainly never been around so many bears
at one time.

But they had nothing worry about. The bungee bears
were so friendly, it was like having a whole zoo full of
best friends.

48

There were lots of fun-fantastic things to do in Cloudville. And before you could spell M-I-S-S-I-S-S-I-P-P-I, the two friends were invited to inner-tube down the huge, winding "cloud slide." They tossed "cloud disks" with the older bears. (Disks are like "Frisbees" that are light as feathers, and sail straight and far every time.) And they especially loved racing the "cloud carts" all over Cloudville! (In Cloudville, because the cloud carts are so soft and safe, you get your driver's license at age 3!)

49

After a long day of playing with their new friends, both Lance and Honey were worn out. They ate a bowl of "cloud broth." (If you've never had any, a single bowl is as filling as a whole dinner.) Then they said "good night" prayers and went to bed. But even as they slept, Lance and Honey were about to be in as much danger as their two friends below them!

Little did Lance and Honey know that exactly two miles straight down from where they slept, Chewy and Giggles were in danger. It was trouble *so* serious, that if they didn't get help soon, it would be their last adventure.

Sharks, Dolphins, and Starfish

When last we saw Giggles and Chewy, they were in a submarine racing full speed toward the ocean floor! They were about to crash, and their trail certainly would have ended in tragedy—if not for one thing.

Beavers *love* instruction books. And they're good at finding and following instructions.

Chewy grabbed Captain Stop's instruction book. In a flash, he flipped to the "all stop!" diagram, which was right where he thought it would be. Chewy pulled the "stop" cord that hung next to the huge fan. The fan did stop . . . but the ship was *still* going too fast!

Chapter Six

"Try to pull up!" cried Chewy, helping Captain Stop pull back on the ship's wheel. (This was something else Chewy had found in the instruction book. Pushing the ship's wheel forward or pulling it back made the submarine go down or up.)

Yet for all their pulling, the submarine would still have smashed to the bottom with a great splintering crash— had it not been for the one thing that happened next. Actually, it was one thing with *two* very positive results.

The first good thing was that they accidentally stopped a terrible crime! In all the commotion of trying to stop the submarine, they didn't notice the huge shark with a mask over his eyes, straight ahead. This shark was the worst kind of shark. In fact, he was filling a large sack with dozens and dozens of baby starfish from their nursery! (He was stealing them for a very mean Walrus who gobbled up the little stars like candy!)

The shark had his sack almost filled to the top with these helpless little stars. In fact, he was just getting ready to put the last few in and tie the top when he looked up.

The last thing this mean shark expected to see was a submarine racing toward him at full speed. The craft landed right on top of him, cushioning the blow so that the submarine landed safely, and freeing the starfish at the same time!

53

"Look at all the stars!" cried Chewy.

"The riddle!" exclaimed Giggles. They hugged each other as they remembered the verse:

"Straight down you will go until you see stars; . . ."

And sure enough, they had done it. Gone *straight down* to where there were stars. As they looked out of the submarine at the starfish nursery, they could see that the baby starfish had been arranged by their mommies in a huge "X." They'd found their "X" marks the spot as well!

With the submarine safely stopped, Captain Stop had gone back to reading the instruction book on how to get them all back to the surface. That's when he read that to reset the "bottom-side-up" button (the one Giggles had pushed), someone would have to go outside into the water.

Everyone knows that chickens can't swim! But otters and beavers (and kids like you) *love* the water. So quick as a wink, the two friends put on scuba gear. Then Captain Stop had them climb into the torpedo tubes (used only for shooting out speeding swimmers on this ship), and shot them outside in a burst of bubbles!

Once outside in the water, Chewy and Giggles quickly freed the rest of the baby starfish, and were surrounded by a host of appreciative mom and dad starfish as well. (The mom and dad starfish had been racing to the rescue the whole time . . . but racing for a starfish is very slow!) Then a whole troop of "Dolphin police" showed up!

Everyone knows that dolphins won't tolerate sharks hurting anyone. That's why they also had been racing to the rescue. But with the rescue already over, to celebrate, the two friends got to play "Race the Dolphins"—the best underwater game they'd ever played.

Giggles the Otter and her curious, fun-loving nature had helped them solve the riddle and make new friends along the way. But Chewy the Beaver's common sense and attention to detail had saved their lives.

Finally it was time to come back inside the submarine. The dolphins did a "one fin" thank you wave and swam off. Chewy and Giggles pushed the reset button. Then they headed for the hatch to get back inside. But before they could make it into the submarine, something happened that would reunite the four friends, bring the two trails together, solve both riddles, and put them all in more danger then they'd ever been in before!

Two Trails
. . . and Two
Worlds Meet

When we last saw Lance and Honey, they'd just had the time of their lives with their new bungee bear friends. (Especially racing those "cloud carts" up and down cloud hills!) They'd played so long and hard, and had so much fun, they'd gone to bed right after dinner. That's when they made a mistake that would bring the four friends back together . . . in a surprising way.

Chapter Seven

Lance and Honey were both tucked into a "bungee bed." A beautiful, fourposter cloud bed, even softer than it sounds. And they were covered up with large, warm blankets, made of extra bungee bear fur. Those blankets make you warm as toast while you dream of birthdays and best friends. In no time, Lance and Honey were fast asleep.

But they forgot to tie the bungee cord on their bed to the cloud. Instead, they tied it to a chest of drawers. The bungee cord is supposed to keep the bed from sliding off the cloud while everyone sleeps . . . *but that's just what happened to Lance and Honey!*

Because bungee bear children all have bungee cords attached to them, a bungee bed falling off the cloud just means losing the bed—not the children. *But Lance and Honey didn't have bungee cords attached to them!*

It was very early morning. The cloud suddenly tilted from a gust of wind. When it did, the bed the two friends were in slid right out the door, down the street, across a field (almost hitting a bungee cow who was munching bungee grass), and right off the cloud into midair, dragging the chest of drawers behind it! Just as they slipped off the cloud, Lance woke up with a big yawn, and then a sudden yell that woke Honey. "We're falling!" he cried. And they were. Like a rock they fell out of the sky!

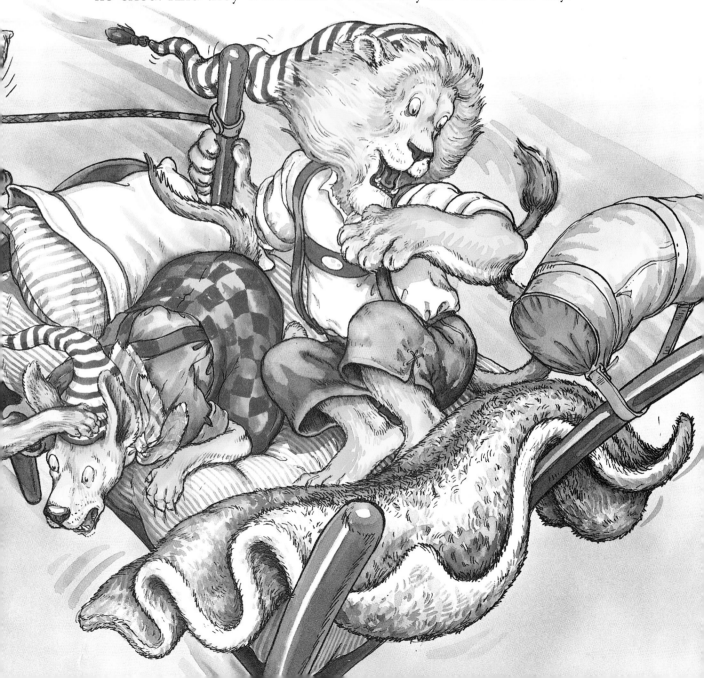

Meanwhile, as Lance and Honey slept their way into
trouble, Giggles and Chewy wished they were dreaming!
For just as they were about to get back into the
submarine, the biggest, hugest,
most gargantuan shark in the
entire ocean came racing
toward them!

He was the big brother of the shark who had tried to
steal all the starfish. And with an underwater growl
you could hear all across the ocean, he charged the
startled friends!

There was no time to get back inside the submarine,
so up . . . up . . . up . . . they shot to the surface. They
broke every otter and beaver swim record in the process.
But the shark stayed right behind them, snapping his
huge teeth!

The two friends would have certainly been lost (along
with any future Treasure Tree Tales) had not something
miraculous happened. Just when Chewy and Giggles
broke the surface, the shark shot his head above the
water too, ready for one final pounce. But just then . . .

All the way from Cloudville, falling like a rock, was—*you guessed it!*—a fourposter bed filled with their friends Lance and Honey!

Guess what happened next. With a "wallop" heard from there to where you live, the bed landed right on top of the massive shark . . . knocking him right out of anyone's adventure, ever again.

Honey and Lance landed in the water with a big splash! And while they had both taken swimming lessons each summer, they couldn't swim as far as otters and beavers. So Lance and Honey would have been in big trouble as they came up sputtering and splashing—but just then a mighty sailing ship came into sight!

They were rescued! *Or at least they thought they were.*

As the ship came toward them, it looked deserted. In fact, as the four friends climbed up its side and onto its deck, not a creature stirred or said hello.

That is until the huge hatch that led to below deck burst open—and out jumped *pirates!* Dozens of pirate rats! They were fully as big as Lance, each carrying a cutlass and looking very mean (and not one of them having brushed his teeth or combed his hair before coming out).

It looked like the two
trails were ending all right . . . in
disaster! For quick as you could say,
*"Tie them up and make them walk the
plank,"* those ratty rats had tied up all four
friends and made them walk to the end of a
long, narrow plank.

As the cold water crashed below them, they did
something that makes even best friends come closer
together. They bowed their heads, and prayed together.
And while the Lord answers some prayers in days or even
longer, this prayer was answered at that very moment.

Just as the meanest looking pirate poked Lance with
his sword and started pushing them all into the water,
there came a screeching, and a shouting, and a tumbling,
and a splashing, the likes of which had never been
heard before.

Just when it looked as if all hope was lost, the sharp-eyed eagle family saw their friends in trouble, sounded the alarm, and swooped to the rescue. The mother eagle dove down and grabbed the cutlass from the paw of the biggest rat, and the baby eagles pushed him into the water. And the eagles weren't the only ones coming to the rescue.

The Dolphin police, with a brave starfish riding on
each one's back, were jumping up and over the ship,
knocking pirates into the ocean with a "bonk" of their
snouts just as if they were knocking away sharks. And the
dolphins weren't alone either! For from out of the sky
came bungee bears!

The bungee bears would drop down, grab a pirate by the back of his shirt, and then as they shot back up into the cloud, which had settled high above the ship, they would let go! This sent the pirate for a tumble from a height even higher then that high dive at the big kids' pool.

From that day until this, the four best friends have never seen anything that compares with the sight of dolphins, eagles, starfish, and bungee bears chasing all the pirates overboard. That is, all except that one last pirate.

Just when it seemed the battle was over, the Captain of the Pirates started toward the best friends. They were still tied up and in great danger. But then everyone heard a funny sound.

It sounded like . . . well . . . it *couldn't* have been, of
course. But it sounded like . . . like . . . a chicken! *And it
was!* Captain Stop had finally gotten the *Bottom-Side-Up*
to surface! In fact, it not only surfaced, it shot out of the
water, shooting starfish torpedoes. They knocked the
Pirate Captain over the side of the ship and right out of
our story.

The dolphins called on a helpful swordfish who sawed away the ropes tying up the four friends. And at last, the "battle" foretold in the riddle had been fought . . . and the adventure was indeed almost over. But not before they had a chance to think of the lessons they had learned.

As Lance, Honey, Giggles, and Chewy hugged and thanked their friends, who should flutter down but Wise Old Owl. And, as usual, he wanted to know what they'd learned from their adventure.

Lance and Honey answered first, for theirs had been the first trail.

"I'm thankful I had someone with a sensitive heart along with me," said Lance. "Without Honey's kindness and understanding, I don't think we'd have become friends with the eagles."

"And without Lance's strength and quick-thinking, we would have been separated when the eagle picked me up and we never would have finished our adventure," said Honey.

"And I'm thankful for Giggles," said Chewy. "We're soooo different—but her joy and happiness gave me hope, even when things looked hopeless."

"And they would have been hopeless without you along, Chewy," said Giggles. "We'd have been stuck in the sand at the bottom of the ocean, if you hadn't figured out a way to make things 'just right.'"

"And I learned how much you all like birthday cake!" said Mother Beaver, who had just rowed alongside. The whole deck of her boat was covered with yummy cakes, some covered with thick chocolate and others with the yummiest strawberry icing.

And so it was, that as they all sat together and swapped stories and yummy cake, Two Trails and Two Worlds came together. They were as different as high and low, clouds and water, eagles and starfish, Lions and Retrievers, and Beavers and Otters. But they all found out that love, courage, prayer, and caring acts can build a bridge across their differences . . . helping them love each other like best friends, as God's friends should.

Personality Checklist

Is your child a Lion, Otter, Golden Retriever, or Beaver? What about you? Read the descriptions out loud. Put your child's or your initial by each description that is a consistent character trait. Total the initials for each personality. The larger numbers indicate basic personality traits.

LION:

1. Is daring and unafraid in new situations.
2. Likes to be a leader. Often tells others how to do things.
3. Ready to take on any kind of challenge.
4. Is firm and serious about what is expected.
5. Makes decisions quickly.

Total = _____

OTTER:

1. Talks a lot and tells wild stories.
2. Likes to do all kinds of fun things.
3. Enjoys being in groups. Likes to perform.
4. Full of energy and always eager to play.
5. Always happy and sees the good part of everything.

Total = _____

GOLDEN RETRIEVER:

1. Always loyal and faithful to friends.
2. Listens carefully to others.
3. Likes to help others. Feels sad when others are hurt.
4. Is a peacemaker. Doesn't like it when others argue.
5. Patient and willing to wait for something.

Total = _____

BEAVER:

1. Is neat, tidy, and notices little details.
2. Sticks with something until it's done. Doesn't like to quit in the middle of a game.
3. Asks lots of questions.
4. Likes things done the same way.
5. Tells things just the way they are.

Total = _____

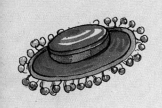